Snuggles the Sleepy Kitten

"It'll be nice having someone living next door again," Mr Chapman remarked.

But Snuggles wasn't listening. He trotted into the living room and curled up on the rug. By the time Mr Chapman had made himself a cup of tea, the kitten was fast asleep again.

Titles in Jenny Dale's KITTEN TALES™ series

All of Jenny Dale's KITTEN TALES books can
be ordered at your local bookshop or are
available by post from Book Service by Post
(tel: 01624 675137)

Snuggles the Sleepy Kitten

by Jenny Dale

Illustrated by Susan Hellard

A Working Partners Book

MACMILLAN CHILDREN'S BOOKS

To Vicky's Tigger

Special thanks to Narinder Dhami

First published 2001 by Macmillan Children's Books
a division of Macmillan Publishers Limited
20 New Wharf Road, London N1 9RR
Basingstoke and Oxford
www.panmacmillan.com

Associated companies throughout the world

Created by Working Partners Limited, London W6 0QT

ISBN 0 330 39734 6

57986

A CIP catalogue record for this book is available from
the British Library.

Typeset by SX Composing DTP, Rayleigh, Essex
Printed and bound in Great Britain by Mackays of Chatham plc, Kent

Chapter One

Super-Snuggles the Wonder Cat
stood very still. His back was
arched, and the tip of his tail
waved slowly from side to side.
Timmy, the biggest fiercest
tomcat in town, was walking
towards him.

Super-Snuggles stared the

ginger tom right in the eyes. One of them would have to move out of the way. Who would it be?

Timmy got closer. And closer . . .

But Super-Snuggles stood his ground. It was about time Timmy treated Super-Snuggles the Wonder Cat with a bit of respect!

"Morning, Super-Snuggles," Timmy miaowed politely. He stepped quickly around the other cat. "And how are you today?"

"Fine," Super-Snuggles purred. "Just fine!"

"*Snuggles . . .*"

The voice was coming from a long way off.

"*Snuggles!*"

Snuggles, the tabby kitten, opened one blue eye. His owner,

Mr Chapman, was stroking his back.

"Goodness, Snuggles, you've been asleep for hours!" Mr Chapman said. "I was beginning to get worried about you."

"I'm OK, Mr Chapman," Snuggles purred. He yawned and stretched, then rubbed his face against Mr Chapman's cardigan. "In fact, I was having a brilliant dream!"

Snuggles *loved* curling up on Mr Chapman's comfy lap and going to sleep. In his dreams he became Super-Snuggles the Wonder Cat . . .

Super-Snuggles could jump high and run fast. All the other cats in town wanted to be like

him. And all the dogs were scared of him. Super-Snuggles could do anything! He could do all the things that Snuggles the kitten was too scared to do.

But Snuggles knew that Mr Chapman worried about him, because he slept so much.

"I can't become Super-Snuggles the Wonder Cat *unless* I'm

asleep!" Snuggles purred, looking up into his owner's kind old face. "I wish I could make you understand."

"Don't go to sleep again, Snuggles," Mr Chapman said anxiously. "Why don't you go and play in the garden for a while?"

Snuggles stopped purring. "The garden!" he mewed worriedly. "What if Timmy the tomcat chases me?" Snuggles was very scared of bad-tempered Timmy – except in his dreams!

"Come on, Snuggles." Mr Chapman picked the kitten up and carried him into the kitchen. "I'll come with you."

Snuggles couldn't help

shivering as his owner unlocked the back door. The outside world seemed such a scary place.

Mr Chapman put Snuggles down on the lawn. The kitten padded slowly across the grass, looking around him worriedly as he went.

Suddenly, Snuggles noticed a small hole in the bottom of the fence. His whiskers twitched with interest. The house on the other side had been empty for as long as Snuggles had lived with Mr Chapman. Snuggles had heard his owner say that its garden had become very overgrown – like a jungle! Snuggles imagined it to be a very frightening place.

But even though he was scared,

the kitten couldn't resist having a
quick peep through the hole. He
poked his stripy face through
and . . .

WHAT WAS THAT?
Something was moving in there!
Snuggles dashed into the house
as fast as his paws could carry
him.

"Snuggles, it's only a blackbird!" Mr Chapman called, as he saw what had frightened his kitten. The bird flew up over the fence and into a tree.

But Snuggles had had enough of the big scary world outside.

Mr Chapman came back in, shaking his head. As soon as he sat down, Snuggles jumped onto his owner's lap and curled up in a tight little ball. It was the only place he felt safe.

"No, Snuggles, don't go to sleep again," Mr Chapman said. "Wake up!"

But Snuggles was already fast asleep.

Chapter Two

"I don't think there's anything to worry about, Mr Chapman," said the vet. She finished examining Snuggles. "He seems fine."

"Of *course* I'm fine," Snuggles mewed, as Mr Chapman put him back into his basket. "I could have told you that!" While his owner was talking to the vet, the kitten snuggled into his blanket and closed his eyes.

By the time they left the surgery, Snuggles was fast asleep . . .

Super-Snuggles the Wonder Cat was prowling round Mr Chapman's back garden. One flick of his tail, and not a single bird even *dared* to land in any of the trees.

Super-Snuggles stared at the fence in between Mr Chapman's garden and the one next door. "I wonder what the other garden's like?" he miaowed to himself.

The fence was very high, but that wasn't a problem for Super-Snuggles the Wonder Cat.

"Here I go!" Super-Snuggles miaowed loudly. He sprang into the air, soared over the fence – and landed safely on the other side. "That was easy!" he purred.

Super-Snuggles looked around the garden. There were lots of tall trees to climb. But best of all, there was a large pond, filled

with plump, orange fish . . .

"*Snuggles*?"

Mr Chapman's voice suddenly popped into the kitten's dream.

"Not now," Super-Snuggles mewed crossly. "I want to explore next door's garden."

"Snuggles, wake up!"

Crossly, Snuggles opened an eye. He didn't *want* to wake up. His dream was too exciting!

"We're home, Snuggles," said Mr Chapman. "And look, a new family is moving in next door."

Snuggles stretched, then sat up in his travelling basket. An enormous lorry was parked in the road. Four men were lifting furniture out of it. A woman was standing in next door's garden with a boy. She had a toddler in her arms – a little girl.

The woman waved at Mr Chapman. "Hello, we're your new neighbours!" she called. "I'm Sue Bourne, and these are my children, Mark and Emily."

"Hello," Mr Chapman called back. "I'm Ron Chapman. And this is my kitten Snuggles." He held up the cat basket.

Snuggles looked at the new people, feeling a bit nervous. They *seemed* friendly, he thought.

"Oh, I love cats!" said Mark. He hurried over to get a closer look at Snuggles. "Hello," he said. He reached through the bars of the basket to tickle Snuggles's head.

"Hello," Snuggles purred back.

"Do you have a cat, Mark?" Mr Chapman asked.

Mark shook his head. "No. But I used to go to my best friend Paul's house and play with his kitten after school. And Mum and Dad have said I can have my own cat when Emily's a bit older," he added eagerly.

"Pussy-cat!" said Emily. She leaned over and tried to grab Snuggles's basket.

"Well, Mark, you're welcome to come and play with Snuggles," Mr Chapman said, smiling.

Mark's face lit up. "Thanks, Mr Chapman."

Snuggles was pleased too. Mark seemed very friendly.

"And you must come and have tea with us, when we've settled in," Mrs Bourne said to Mr Chapman.

"Can Snuggles come too, Mum?" Mark asked quickly.

"Of course!" his mum agreed.

CRASH!

Snuggles almost leaped out of his basket as one of the removal men dropped a box onto the pavement. He wriggled under his blanket and lay there out of sight, shaking with fear.

"Oh dear!" Mrs Bourne groaned. "Well, it was nice to meet you, Mr Chapman." She hurried out of the garden to inspect the box.

"And nice to meet you too, Snuggles!" Mark added.

Snuggles gingerly poked his head out to mew goodbye.

"Well, the Bournes seem very friendly, don't they, Snuggles?" Mr Chapman remarked. He carried Snuggles into the house, then let him out of his basket. "It'll be nice to have someone living next door again."

But Snuggles wasn't listening. He trotted into the living room and curled up on the rug.

By the time Mr Chapman had made himself a cup of tea, the kitten was fast asleep again. "Oh, *Snuggles*!" Mr Chapman sighed. "What *am* I going to do with you?"

Chapter Three

"And you be careful with those boxes!" Super-Snuggles the Wonder Cat miaowed. He kept a stern eye on the removal men going in and out of the house next door. "They belong to my friend Mark, and I'll be very cross if you drop them!"

The removal men were carrying the boxes very slowly and carefully into the house.

"Good!" Super-Snuggles purred. "Just remember that I'm watching you . . ."

"Snuggles, you'll have to get off my lap."

Snuggles opened his eyes to find Mr Chapman gently lifting him up.

"There's someone at the door," Mr Chapman went on, putting the kitten down on the carpet.

Snuggles yawned. "I was having a brilliant dream," he mewed sleepily. "I really made those removal men behave themselves!"

Mr Chapman went to answer

the door.

Snuggles padded after him, and saw their new neighbour standing on the doorstep. "Hello, Mark!" he purred happily.

"Hello, Mr Chapman," Mark said. "We were wondering if you and Snuggles would like to come round and have tea with us."

"Well, that's very kind of you," Mr Chapman said, looking very pleased.

Mark beamed. "Can I carry Snuggles over to my house, please?" he asked hopefully.

Mr Chapman nodded. So Mark carefully scooped the kitten into his arms.

Snuggles cuddled nervously against his new friend. He didn't really like going outside the house.

As they walked down Mr Chapman's path, a dog in one of the nearby houses began to bark loudly.

Snuggles stiffened in alarm. "Uh-oh!" he hissed. "It's big Barney! I've seen him walk past our garden – he's really fierce!" He tried to scramble down the neck of Mark's sweatshirt.

"That's Barney the Alsatian," Mr Chapman explained to Mark. "He belongs to Mr Gordon at Number 21. I'm afraid Snuggles is a bit scared of him."

"No, I'm not!" Snuggles mewed indignantly. "Well, maybe just a tiny bit . . ."

*

When they were safely inside Mark's house, Snuggles felt much happier. He looked around curiously. All the furniture was in place now, but there were still lots of cardboard boxes to be unpacked.

"Let's play in the garden, Snuggles," Mark suggested.

"We've got time before tea."

"The *garden*?" Snuggles mewed, his eyes wide. Go into that scary, dark, overgrown garden? He wasn't sure he liked that idea very much . . .

Mark unlocked the back door and carried Snuggles outside. He gently put the kitten down on the path, then ran off down the overgrown lawn. "Come on, Snuggles!" he called, taking a small rubber ball from his pocket. "Bet you can't get to the ball before I do!" He threw the ball across the garden.

"I bet I can!" Snuggles miaowed. Without thinking, he raced into the grass – which was almost as tall as he was. He found the ball and pounced down on top of it, so that it was hidden under his fat, furry little tummy.

Mark laughed. "That's cheating, Snuggles!"

"Oh, all right," Snuggles mewed, and stood up. But when Mark bent down to pick the ball up, Snuggles batted it smartly with his paw. The ball rolled away across the grass, out of Mark's reach.

"Snuggles, stop it!" Mark laughed. This time he grabbed the ball before the kitten reached it, and threw it across the lawn again.

Snuggles rushed after the ball so quickly he did a somersault, and landed SPLAT! on his bottom.

"Oh, Snuggles, you're so funny!" Mark grinned.

"Maybe, but I've got the ball!" Snuggles purred, batting it away from Mark again with his paw.

Snuggles was quite amazed. The garden wasn't as scary as he'd thought! It *was* a bit dark and overgrown, but he didn't feel frightened – because Mark was playing in it too.

Mark took Snuggles to explore the wild patch at the bottom of the garden. They hid behind trees and jumped out at each other. They even rolled around in a big pile of grass cuttings. Then Mark fetched some empty cardboard boxes. He built a big tower and helped Snuggles to climb all the way to the top.

Snuggles really enjoyed playing with his new friend. But after a while he began to feel a bit strange – as though he had forgotten something important . . .

Then he remembered. "Oh!" he mewed. "My afternoon nap!"

The kitten began to make his

way back up the garden, towards the house.

"Snuggles?" Mark called, puzzled. "What's the matter?"

"I almost forgot to have my afternoon Super-Snuggles adventure!" Snuggles mewed. He went through the open back door and into the Bournes' living room.

Mr Chapman was sitting on the sofa, talking to Emily, who was in her playpen. Mrs Bourne was laying out cups and plates for tea.

Snuggles leaped up onto his owner's lap, then settled down and closed his eyes.

"I see what you mean about Snuggles sleeping a lot, Mr

Chapman!" Mark's mum said, smiling.

Mr Chapman sighed as he stroked his kitten's head.

"Where's Snuggles?" Mark asked, coming into the living room. "Oh!"

Snuggles was almost asleep by now, but he could hear that Mark sounded a bit disappointed.

"We were having a great game," Mark went on.

Yes, we were, thought Snuggles sleepily. He liked playing with Mark. In fact, playing with Mark was *almost* as much fun as a Super-Snuggles dream . . .

Chapter Four

Super-Snuggles stood outside
Number 21, his tail waving
angrily from side to side. Inside
the house, a dog was barking
loudly.

"That Barney!" Super-Snuggles
hissed crossly. "He's always
barking. It's time someone sorted

him out!"

The garden gate was shut. It was quite high, but that didn't stop Super-Snuggles. He leaped over it, and strolled up the garden path. The front door of Number 21 was shut, but a window at the side of the house was open. Super-Snuggles jumped onto the windowsill and looked inside.

Barney the Alsatian was standing in the kitchen. "In case anyone has forgotten, I'M in charge around here," he barked. "This is MY—" Barney stopped when he saw Super-Snuggles glaring at him through the window. "Er . . . hello, Super-Snuggles," he woofed – *much* more quietly. "Is something wrong?"

"There certainly is," Super-Snuggles miaowed coolly. He stepped through the window and onto the draining board, his whiskers twitching.

Barney looked a bit nervous. "What?" he woofed.

"There's an annoying dog in my street who never stops barking!" Super-Snuggles hissed, staring hard at Barney.

The big dog bared his teeth. "Grr! You tell me who's annoying you, Super-Snuggles, and I'll see him off!" he growled.

Really! Super-Snuggles thought. *Dogs are so stupid!* "The dog's name is Barney, and he lives at Number 21," he miaowed.

"Right!" Barney barked. Then he looked puzzled. "Hang on a minute, that's *me*, isn't it?"

Super-Snuggles jumped down onto the kitchen floor, stalked over to the Alsatian and looked him in the eye. "Yes, it is," he miaowed.

Barney's ears and tail drooped. "Sorry. I'll never bark loudly again, Super-Snuggles!" he whimpered. "I promise . . ."

"That's Mark at the door!"

Hearing this, Snuggles left Super-Snuggles telling Barney off, and woke up. He jumped off Mr Chapman's lap and raced down the hall.

It was a few days since Snuggles and Mr Chapman had gone to tea at the Bournes' house. And Mark had called in to play with the kitten every afternoon when he got home from school.

Snuggles really enjoyed the lively games they played. Kind

old Mr Chapman had the comfiest lap in the world, but he couldn't run around the garden with Snuggles like Mark did.

"Hello, Mark," Snuggles purred, as Mr Chapman opened the door. The kitten launched himself at Mark and pounced on the laces of his trainers. It was one of his favourite games.

"Hi, Mr Chapman," Mark grinned. "Can I have my laces back, please, Snuggles? I need them to keep my trainers on!"

"Why?" Snuggles grabbed one of the laces in his teeth and shook it from side to side. "I don't know why people wear such smelly shoes anyway!"

"Snuggles, behave yourself!" Mr Chapman laughed. "Come in, Mark."

"Race you to the back door, Mark!" Snuggles miaowed happily. And he shot off down the hall, with Mark chasing after him.

When Mr Chapman had unlocked the back door, Snuggles and Mark ran out into the garden.

Snuggles had almost forgotten that he'd ever been scared of going outside. Now he and Mark went out whenever the weather was fine.

It was a crisp, bright autumn day. Red and gold leaves were falling gently from the trees onto the lawn.

"Come on, Mark!" Snuggles mewed. "Let's catch the leaves for a while!" He jumped up at a leaf as it floated down towards him and batted it with his paw.

"Well done, Snuggles!" Mark called. Then he looked around the garden. "I feel like climbing a tree," he said.

Snuggles's heart sank. "I'm too scared to climb trees," he mewed quietly. "Only Super-Snuggles can do that."

Mark pointed at the tallest tree in Mr Chapman's garden. "Come on, Snuggles. Let's climb that one!"

Snuggles looked nervously at the tree. It was so tall, it seemed to go on for ever. Even Super-Snuggles hadn't climbed it yet. Snuggles was sure *he'd* never be able to climb the tree. Not even with Mark's help.

"I'll give you a hand, Snuggles." Mark picked up the kitten and, standing on tiptoe, placed him on one of the lower branches. "Now just wait there while I climb up to you."

"I'm not going anywhere!"

Snuggles mewed in a scared voice. "Help!" The kitten was very frightened indeed. He felt as though he was going to fall off any minute. He didn't like it at all.

"Mark, your mum's here," Mr Chapman called from the back door. Snuggles was *very* relieved.

"OK," Mark called back. He lifted Snuggles off the branch. "The tree will have to wait until tomorrow," he said. Then he gave the kitten a cuddle as he carried him back into the house.

Snuggles was still feeling a bit shaky, so he decided to go and have a nap. A Super-Snuggles adventure would make him feel better.

Mr Chapman was busy in the kitchen, so the kitten curled up on the rug in front of the fire. What would Super-Snuggles do today? he wondered. He'd have to wait and see . . .

Super-Snuggles the Wonder Cat sat on the front garden fence, watching all the dogs in the street walking up and down. They hardly made a sound.

"Hello, Super-Snuggles," Barney woofed very softly, trotting up to him. "I've told all the other dogs not to bark loudly any more, because it annoys you."

"Thanks, Barney," Super-Snuggles miaowed.

The Alsatian wagged his tail happily.

Super-Snuggles sat and watched all the dogs woofing to each other really, really quietly. It was great fun!

Or was it?

"Just a minute," Super-Snuggles mewed, feeling rather miserable. "Something's not quite right here . . ."

Snuggles stirred in his sleep, beginning to wake up. *What is the matter with Super-Snuggles?* he thought drowsily. *Why does he feel so fed up?*

"Snuggles, wake up." Mr Chapman came into the living room carrying a sandwich and a cup of tea. "Were you asleep again? I sometimes wonder what you dream about!"

"Oh, I always have *great* dreams, Mr Chapman," Snuggles miaowed, yawning. "Being Super-Snuggles the Wonder Cat is the most fun ever!" But then he sat up and thought hard. His dream hadn't felt quite so exciting today.

Snuggles felt a bit upset. He could hardly eat any of the tuna that Mr Chapman offered him.

What was the matter with him? He always *loved* being Super-Snuggles in his dreams. So why hadn't he enjoyed *this* dream? What had changed?

The kitten decided to go back to sleep. Maybe he could find out.

Chapter Five

Super-Snuggles bounded over the fences into every garden in the street. At Number 21, Barney was waiting for him.

"Hello, Super-Snuggles," Barney woofed quietly. "Welcome to my garden. I've got a big fish for you from my owner's fridge."

"Thanks." Super-Snuggles ate the fish and then leaped over the fence into the next garden.

Mrs Foster's Boxer, Jason, was sitting there with a whole roast chicken in front of him. "I hope you like it, Super-Snuggles," he woofed politely.

"It will do," Super-Snuggles

miaowed. And he ate the whole lot. Then he jumped over two more fences into the garden of Number 27, where Mr Lane's mongrel, Sally, had a pork chop waiting for him.

"You're my hero, Super-Snuggles," Sally woofed, wagging her tail at him.

"Hang on a minute." Super-Snuggles sat down. "Something's not right here," he mewed miserably.

"Oh no! It's happening again!" Snuggles miaowed as he woke up. It had been a great dream – all the scary dogs in the street giving Super-Snuggles his favourite food!

But Super-Snuggles just wasn't

enjoying himself any more. And Snuggles didn't know why.

"Snuggles, what's wrong?" Mr Chapman put down his newspaper and gently scratched the kitten's head. "You don't look very happy."

"I'm not!" Snuggles mewed miserably. No matter what Super-Snuggles did, the dreams weren't so exciting. They didn't feel very *real*.

But Snuggles was determined not to give up. "Maybe I should sleep even *more*," he mewed. "Then I might be able to get my lovely, exciting dreams back!"

Snuggles thought that this was a really good idea. So he curled up on Mr Chapman's lap again.

"Oh, Snuggles, you're not going to sleep *again*!" Mr Chapman exclaimed. "You've only just woken up!"

Just then the doorbell rang.

"Aren't you coming to see who it is, Snuggles?" Mr Chapman asked. He lifted the kitten off his lap and slowly stood up. "It might be Mark."

"I can't," Snuggles miaowed, keeping his eyes tightly shut. "I *have* to have a really good dream . . ."

"Hi, Mr Chapman."

Snuggles recognised Mark's voice. The kitten longed to rush into the hall and say hello. But he stayed where he was.

"Mum wants to know if you

and Snuggles would like to come to lunch today," Mark went on.

"We'd love to," Mr Chapman agreed. "If I can wake Snuggles up, that is!"

"Oh, is he asleep again?" said Mark, coming into the living room.

Snuggles kept his eyes closed and pretended to be asleep, even when Mark crouched down to stroke him.

"Don't you want to play, Snuggles?" Mark sounded very disappointed.

Snuggles felt guilty about not getting up to play with his friend. But he didn't move.

"Never mind, Mark," said Mr Chapman. "You'll be able to play

with Snuggles when we come over for lunch."

"OK," said Mark. But he still sounded upset. "Mum says to come over at about one o'clock." Then he went back next door.

Snuggles felt very mean. He didn't want to make Mark unhappy. He loved Mark nearly as much as he loved Mr

Chapman, now.

The kitten decided that he would play with Mark all afternoon to make it up to him. "But now I *must* get to sleep," he sighed.

Super-Snuggles stood looking up at the huge tree. Its branches stretched right up into the sky. It was a long way to the top, but Super-Snuggles knew he could do it.

He began to climb. He leaped lightly from branch to branch, getting higher with every jump. The tree swayed gently in the breeze, but that didn't worry Super-Snuggles the Wonder Cat. He just kept right on going.

"I did it!" Super-Snuggles miaowed, as he jumped up onto the highest branch. "I climbed the tallest tree!"

It should have been one of the best dreams ever.

"But it isn't," Super-Snuggles miaowed sadly. He looked down into next door's garden. Mark was out there, playing with his little sister. He was chasing her round the garden, and they were laughing happily.

"You know what?" Super-Snuggles the Wonder Cat miaowed. "I wish *I* could play with Mark!"

Chapter Six

"OH!" Snuggles woke up with a jolt.

"Snuggles!" Mr Chapman was staring at his kitten, looking puzzled. "You made me jump! What's the matter?"

"It's OK, Mr Chapman," Snuggles mewed. "*Now* I know

why my Super-Snuggles adventures aren't such fun any more."

Mr Chapman stared down at his excited little kitten. "What on *earth* is the matter with you, Snuggles?"

"My real world is more exciting than my dream world, now that I've got Mark to play with!" Snuggles explained happily.

He jumped off Mr Chapman's lap, and charged to the front door, tail waving madly. "I'm tired of dreaming. Can we go and see Mark now?"

"Snuggles, what's the matter?" Mr Chapman came out into the hall. "Don't scratch the door!"

"*Please*, Mr Chapman," Snuggles

mewed.

Mr Chapman picked up his kitten, then looked at his watch. "Let's go next door," he said. "It's nearly time for lunch. And at least that will stop you scratching my front door to pieces!"

As Mr Chapman carried Snuggles outside, the kitten's heart thumped with excitement.

How could he have thought that silly old dreams could be better than having *real* adventures, playing with Mark?

Mark was looking out for them. His face lit up and he dashed outside to open the front gate.

Mr Chapman handed Snuggles to him.

The kitten rubbed his furry cheek against Mark's. "Sorry, Mark," he purred. "Playing with *you* is the best fun ever!"

"*Woof! Woof!*"

Snuggles turned round and saw Barney the Alsatian walking down the street with his owner.

"Grr!" Barney had spotted Snuggles, and was trying to pull his owner towards him. "I don't like cats!" he growled fiercely.

Snuggles's fur bristled in fear. But he couldn't let smelly old Barney spoil his fun with Mark. He knew he had to be brave. What would Super-Snuggles do?

The kitten arched his back and lowered his ears, hoping it made him look fierce. "You'd better not talk to me like that, Barney," he hissed. "Or I'll chase you right up the street!"

Barney was so surprised that he stopped barking at once.

"You showed *him*, Snuggles!" Mark laughed, as he carried the kitten inside.

"Yes, I did, didn't I?" Snuggl purred, rather surprised h

There were deliciou

coming from the kitchen which made Snuggles's whiskers twitch.

"Let's go into the garden, Snuggles." Mark put the kitten down, and went to open the back door. "I'll show you my new tree house."

"Great!" Snuggles purred happily.

Mark's tree house was perched in the branches of the tallest tree in the Bournes' garden. Snuggles could see that the tree was even taller than the one Super-Snuggles had climbed in Mr _oman's garden. There was a _dder leading up to the tree

Snugg_

_ you up there, _asked, bending

to pick the kitten up.

"No," Snuggles miaowed bravely. He shrugged away Mark's hand. "I'm going to *climb* up the tree – just like Super-Snuggles would!"

"You'll never get up there!" someone miaowed rudely.

Snuggles turned round and saw Timmy the tomcat perched on the fence, his tail swinging.

"Oh yes, I will!" Snuggles mewed back. It was funny – he didn't feel scared of Timmy at *all* now!

Mark began to climb up the ladder and Snuggles scrambled up the tree trunk behind him. It wasn't easy and his legs were tired out before he was halfway there. But he kept going.

The sun was warm on the kitten's back. A gentle breeze ruffled his fur. "I did it!" Snuggles miaowed, as he finally reached the tree house.

He could see all the streets and gardens for miles around. He was so close to the blue sky that he

felt as if he could reach out with his paw and touch it.

Snuggles thought that this was better than *any* of his Super-Snuggles dreams. He wasn't scared at all, now that he'd got used to the swaying movements of the tree. But best of all, Mark was there too.

Snuggles and Mark played in the tree house until lunch was ready.

Then Mrs Bourne called them in, and everyone sat down to a huge roast chicken, with lots of potatoes, vegetables and gravy.

Snuggles had his own special bowl under the table, which was full of small pieces of meat. And Mark kept slipping him more bits too! Snuggles had never been so full in his life.

After lunch, Snuggles curled up on Mr Chapman's lap and yawned. He was tired out from all their energetic games and from eating so much food.

"Look, Snuggles is going to sleep again," laughed Mrs Bourne.

"Well, I think he deserves a nap this time," Mr Chapman smiled.

"Yes, he's been awake for ages," agreed Mark.

"Don't worry, Mr Chapman," Snuggles mewed. "I'm not going to sleep for long. As soon as my tummy's not so full, I'm going out with Mark to climb another tree!"